MW01526387

Cyberpunk Fairy Tales: Volume 1

Cyberpunk Fairy Tales, Volume 1

George Saoulidis

Published by Mythography Studios, 2019.

CYBERPUNK FAIRY TALES: VOLUME 1

First edition. January 9, 2019.

Copyright © 2019 George Saoulidis.

ISBN: 978-1386523772

Written by George Saoulidis.

Also by George Saoulidis

Antigravel
Where a Spaceship Goes to Die
Girl Gone Nova
Cosmophobia
Antigravel Omnibus 1

A Thousand Eves
A Thousand Eves

Cyberpink
Hewoo
Berenice's Hair
Come and Get It
Kimono Coconut

Cyberpunk Fairy Tales
Cyberpunk Fairy Tales: Volume 1
The Impossible Quest of Hailing a Taxi on Christmas Eve

Nanodaemons: The Fir Smart-Tree
The Little Match Girl

Deimos Çelik
Big, Round Snowballs: A GameLit Story

God Complex Universe
Myth Gods Tech 1 - Omnibus Edition: Science Fiction Meets Greek
Mythology In The God Complex Universe
Myth Gods Tech 2 - Omnibus Edition: Science Fiction Meets Greek
Mythology In The God Complex Universe
Bird's-Eye View of the Back of Your Head
Black Asklepios
Erinyes
Boo! A Halloween Story
Life Coach
You Have Too Many Friends
The Whale on the Veil
On Pointe All Day Long

Graft vs Host
Amok|Koma

Hire a Muse
Crying Over Spilt Light
Slow Up

The Road Demands Tribute
The Girl Who Twisted Fate's Arm

Standalone
Frivolous Fox Diligent Dog
Astropithecus
Lightshow Bright
Space Them Out
The Redjus
A Trillion-Dollar Rock
Explosive Decompression
Generations of Gold
Sweet, Hot Taffy
You Say Witch Like It's a Bad Thing: Thea
Gorgonise Me
Speaking in Bubbles
Gorgoneion
MOAB: Mother Of All Boxsets
The Halloween Raid: A GameLit Short Story

Watch for more at https://www.mythographystudios.com/join.

Table of Contents

A Taxi On Christmas Eve
A modern retelling of
"A Christmas Carol"
By Charles Dickens

• • • •

Stave One

"MARLEY WAS DEAD: TO begin with. There is no doubt whatever about that," he read out loud from the first page and then shut the book closed. He exhaled, a puff of frozen breath forming in front of his mouth and said, "And this is supposed to be a fairytale? How morbid."

He held the book in his hands, a real, physical print of "A Christmas Carol" by Charles Dickens. It was only a mass-produced cheap copy but it was vintage enough in this time and age. His late partner had left it on his desk, with a handwritten dedication for him. Scrooge never figured out why.

His name wasn't really Scrooge of course. He was John.

People just called him like that, and the nickname stuck. It was just that every Christmas Eve since his business partner's death on the exact same day, he was reminded of the man. Scrooge didn't have any pictures or anything, just the worn old book in his drawer. He never got to read the thing, it was too dour. He just held it in his hands, feeling the paper, thinking. There's something about the texture of books that appeals to people. The shiny, glossy surfaces of the reading devices nowadays just don't evoke anything similar.

Across the freezing office was his assistant, Clara. She was a single mother of one, in her late thirties and needed a new dye of blonde hair. She could have been attractive, if she had managed to get some sleep, enough money to pay her bills and a miracle to lift the worry off her shoulders. She was an accountant, the only employee to Scrooge, and she ended up juggling every single job, manning the phones, doing the accounts, fixing technical issues with the techs, keeping the office livable with a couple of plants.

She was currently rolled up in a blanket like a gyro wrap, shaking and sniffing her nose. The frigid office was dark, illuminated only by the lights outside, some colourful ones from the Christmas decorations, others simply street signs and lamp-posts, and also by the computer monitors on their desks. She was wearing knit colourful gloves and was tapping away on her phone, constantly stopping to check out something on her monitor by pressing a button, sighing, and then turning back to her phone. It was doing gling sounds all the time, filled with incoming and outgoing Christmas wishes to old friends and faraway family. The glove tips wouldn't normally work on the touchscreen, but she had those popular touchscreen gloves with capacitive elements sewn in the fingers. It was a small comfort in the cold office.

"Mr. Tsifoutis, it's still not working," she nagged to no one in particular.

"The server works half the time, so it's good enough. How many hours do you need to input a few accounts woman?" Scrooge grunted, his eyes not lifting towards her.

"But I'm waiting for over an hour to finish this up and go home. The IT isn't responding, they must have left the office for Christmas Eve." She sniffed her nose. In the beginning, she was trying to do it quietly, discreet like a lady should, but after years and years of enduring a winter office she had just given up and pretty much blew her nose like a loud trumpet.

"Bah! Customer service they call it! It's the same thing every Christmas, you just can't get any work done anywhere," Scrooge spat out, his face turning sour.

"People just want to go home to their families Mr. Tsifoutis," she explained softly.

He got the hint. "Days off with pay... In my day, you could work 14 hours a day 7 days a week and not get paid till four months later," he said shaking his finger.

She waited calmly for him to finish his rant, pulling up the blanket in a futile quest to make herself warm.

"Christmas! Bah! Nothing but a marketing ploy, I tell you. Selling Christmas ornaments and Christmas gifts two full months before the holiday itself. And the waste of it all! The city lights, paid with my taxes. Stupid snow frosting on buildings, requiring money to put on and then money to clean off! A waste. They slap a Christmas packaging on products and mark-up the price by 30%!"

"Thirty percent," she nodded patiently.

He still had more coming but he suddenly felt tired, so he sagged back into his chair. The back was worn and some screws were poking out of the lower back, making it really uncomfortable. He didn't spare any cash to get new office chairs of course. They were fine and sturdy, they still had at least 10 years of good use. "Anyway, go home. I'll finish up here and upload it in a while. You're gonna drain my account anyway, you can have the day off tomorrow."

She stood up and smiled, putting her stuff in her bag, arranging her desk, pulling down the blinds.

Scrooge grunted at her, "But I want you here the next day half an hour earlier!"

"Yes mister," she said, and watered the plants, cleaned up her cup of tea, picked up his cup and put a new cup of water in the boiler. She left it boiling, cleaned up the tiny little kitchen, went to turn off the Christmas lights she had brought to decorate the office, remembered Mr. Scrooge had already demanded her to stop wasting power and turned it off, went back to her desk and sent the accounts of the day to her boss, went to his desk, threw away the trash, dusted off his hanging coat, leaned to his computer, pulled up the accounts so he could update them as soon as the server was running again, went back to the kitchen, poured hot tea, brought it to his desk savouring its warmth for a second too long, stood in front of his desk ready to leave and then said goodnight.

"Good night Clara," Scrooge said with the tone a boss has when he allows his employee to leave.

"Maybe we should do the upgrade Mr. Tsifoutis," she said hesitantly. "Our service depends on it, it's been years. I've shown you the cost, it's not that high and..."

Scrooge raised his hand interrupting her, "I know. I'll think about it."

She was referring to their service, which was their object of trade really. Scrooge was running an accounting internet service for small businesses. Despite that their platform hadn't been updated in, pretty much ever, they were still competitive due to their low prices. The cost was kept down of course, by skimping on things like proper furniture, internet hosting, required employees and, office heating.

"Merry Christmas sir," she said cordially and turned to the door.

"Bah. A marketing ploy I tell you. Don't you listen to anything I say woman?"

"Of course I do, but Merry Christmas anyways," she said and she meant it.

As she was opening the door, Scrooge's cousin showed up. He was fat and huge and was always huffing from exertion, making his cheeks red. He made a great Santa Claus, so he showed up in costume. "Hello Miss Clara! Merry Christmas to you," he said and presented a small gift to her. "For your son." Then he reached into his red Santa bag and fished out a party horn as well.

"Merry Christmas Mr. Tsifoutis," she smiled back. "I'm sure he'll love it."

"Ho ho ho!" the cousin bellowed out and then leaned in to whisper, "Is Scrooge still here?"

"Yes," she replied, "Go right in, he's just waiting for the system to unfreeze."

"Unfreeze? Why, in this cold it might take some time," he said with jolly, half-stepping in the office.

She sneezed and then blew her nose loudly like a trumpet, that echoed into the corridors. Cousin Santa blew his own party horn in a similar note.

They both laughed and wished each other happy holidays.

• • • •

SCROOGE HID HIS FACE in his palms. He didn't really want to face his cousin, he was dodging his invite for days.

The cousin Santa came in and bellowed, "Ho ho ho dear cousin!" and blew his party horn, in a loud *prrr*. He then went to the decorated Christmas lights and turned them on, illuminating the place in various flickering colours.

Scrooge stood up and ran to the lights, turning them off. "Are you trying to bankrupt me man?"

"Come on, a few LEDs wont make a real difference. Be merry! Be jolly!" he said, blowing his party horn and turning the Christmas lights on again.

Scrooge turned them off. "Bah! It's just a marketing ploy."

Santa turned them on. "Will you come to our Christmas dinner tomorrow?"

Scrooge turned them off. "No. I have work to do at home. Clara won't be coming to work tomorrow, I have to keep up the pace."

Santa turned them on. "You can't possibly work on Christmas Day! Come to us for dinner. There'll be turkey! And sweets! And chocolate. We'll have a merry old time..."

Scrooge turned them off. "A waste, overpriced dinners when you can't afford them. Don't be coming to me for loans in a few weeks."

He was referring of course, to actual loans. He'd never lent out money just like that, not even to family, whatever little of both he had left. They were actual personal loans, signed in triplicate, incurring interest at "market average" rates.

Santa sighed and gave up. "Fine. I know you've seen my invitation days ago. I know the message I left to Clara was passed to you. This is just some excuse, I don't know why you don't want to spend the holiday with family. Anyway, the offer stands. Our door is always open for you," he said, blew out the party horn one last time, though it was something sad this time, and left.

• • • •

SCROOGE SHUT THE DOOR and sat back down to his uncomfortable office chair. He pressed a button on his computer and waited for the server to respond. It took more than two minutes for it to spit out an "error: unreachable" message.

It was fine. He could wait. The hosting service he used was the cheapest one there is, and that meant it was poorly maintained and came with customer support that didn't really care.

He picked up the tea, that was scalding hot when Clara brought it but now was barely warmer than the freezing room, and sipped, while staring outside into the dark Christmas Athens. It was still afternoon but it was already pitch going for black.

• • • •

SOMEONE KNOCKED ON the door and he stood up, protesting loudly all the way. "What now? I told you I won't come to the damn dinner," he mumbled and opened the door.

He looked down and saw three little children, fluffed out with big coloured coats and knit caps and gloves. The girl was Romani, the boy was Greek and the second boy was Nigerian.

They cheered in unison, "Na ta poume?" which was the protocol of Christmas Carol initiation. They didn't really have the patience to wait for a proper reply so they began jingling away their little triangles and singing.

It was so merry and sweet.

Scrooge yelled at them and shushed them. "Stop this racket! Stop at once. Who told you to start with this cacophony?"

They extended their little gloved hands and waited for their treat. Their paycard was in hand, a simple tap from another would confirm a small-amount transaction instantly.

"I'm not giving you anything, you little extortionists! Coming here uninvited, mangling out a couple of verses and then demanding payment. No. And you, aren't you a Muslim?" he said and pointed at the little Roma girl.

"We like Christmas, it's a time for family and happiness," she replied with her sweet little voice. "That's what mommy says," she added.

Scrooge squinted. "Do you know how insane that is? Celebrating the birth of Christ from another religion? Tell your mother that I won't be fooled by those pigtails and those big round eyes. A fine scam, if you ask me. Getting money every year without a receipt," he nodded.

The children looked at one another, but since they were stuffed like turkeys they had to turn their whole bodies to exchange glances. They kept their hands up, paycards in hand, but a little lower now.

"And you," Scrooge said, pointing at the Nigerian boy. "What are you?"

The little black boy shrugged. "I'm Greek mister."

"So you are Orthodox Christian?"

"Yes sir. My name is Nico, from the Saint Nicholas," the boy replied, the words repeated by heart. He gifted the bitter man a shiny-white smile that could melt your heart and fill you up with hope.

"Blasted immigrants," Scrooge said and slammed the door to their face.

• • • •

SCROOGE SAT ON HIS desk and hit the button once again. His accounting service attempted to connect for two whole minutes and then spat out an error.

He exhaled, his breath visible in the air. He picked up the phone, but all he got was a recorded message. His assistant had already tried that of course. He thought he wouldn't mind waiting for the server to reconnect, but the absence of a specific timeframe made him weary. If he had known of a general amount of time it might take, he would be willing to wait. But alas, this seemed it would keep him up till the morning.

Scrooge grunted and searched his emails for the long overdue report of the service upgrade that was necessary. He didn't print it of course, toner was so damn expensive, as if it were made of gold particles. Also, what about the environment? Yes, digital files are nice and cheap. He put on his glasses and read the report his late business partner had left him.

It explained in detail the steps necessary to upgrade the accounting service, to improve speed, customer experience and unlock some new features. It was all ready and done, but it wasn't yet needed for a company this small, as it was when his partner was alive. As poor Marco fell increasingly ill, the business growth was halted and was left on the shoulders of Scrooge. He could manage just fine thank you, but regarding the computer and technical aspects it was all on his partner. Scrooge had shopped around for another computer engineer, and they had all asked for an arm and a leg in cash. Marco in his last days, stir-crazy from lying in bed all day, had prepared the system update for when the company would pick up pace again.

The problem was, that the upgrade demanded even more powerful servers, some shiny new gear with fancy names and numbers, all costing more and more and more. Scrooge had been postponing the upgrade for a long time. He checked the report's date. Seven years? Has it really been so long? Marco had planned for a year after his death, but Scrooge hadn't changed anything for six more years, to the dismay of their customers and Miss Clara.

Scrooge rubbed his chin and his hand hovered over the mouse. He never did things in haste, but now, for some reason, something was itching him. He clicked the long-forgotten button in their system and initiated the update program his partner had set-up as his last contribution.

The computer began to process things, as it always does and Scrooge relaxed, sure that the process was a lengthy one.

Where the program ran, a face appeared in a video. Scrooge had to straighten his glasses to see better and for a second he held his breath. He hadn't seen that face in so long, but it was clearly... Marco's face.

Marco's face was staring at him patiently. Then he moved slightly, and Scrooge realised that the video had already began and Marco was simply staring at his own monitor. He was pale and sickly, illuminated harshly by the room-lamp and the monitor. His eyes were sunken, his lips a thin line. These had been his final days.

Marco cleared his throat. "Oh, it's on? Hello Scrooge. You do know of course, that it's by that nickname that people are referring to you. I suspect you know, but don't really care since it empowers your reputation as being tough in business. Anyway, they are referring of course to Disney's Scrooge McDuck, from those old cartoons. The character though, comes from an older archetypal character, that of Ebenezer Scrooge, in the book I have left for you in my office. It is a remarkable tale, centuries old that has seeped into our minds. You and I are pragmatists, I know that I can't really scare you into changing your ways. That Scrooge, a stingy bitter old man, was visited by three spirits, that showed him the Christmas past, present and yet to come. There are no spirits to do the same to you, but I hope that this message of me one year after my death will bear the gravitas necessary to sink in your thoughts. Please, my invaluable partner, please, read it and think about your own life. As I lay here in my bed, between feeling ill from medicine that was meant to make me well and vomiting from the medicine that combat the first one's side-effects, I have had a long time to think my life over. Money is not all there is in this life. The truly precious stuff can't be bought. And if you have them, treasure them while you can because time is fleeting. By now, I assume your business acumen has brought our company - *your* company I guess - to its previous positive profitability. I know you like to keep a tight leash on expenses and that sometimes drives a wedge between you and people, so please don't do that. Do not make the same mistakes I did. Do not die alone. It's still early, there is still time to change your fate. Merry Christmas, dear friend."

The video ended and Scrooge lay silent, staring at the paused digital ghost. Marco had been more than his business partner. He was his friend, he trusted him with finances, with decisions that would affect both their lives. What little competition there was between them was nothing but a game, a nod from one to another to push forward, to do good business deals, to bring in more customers, to make more money. For both of them.

He hadn't expected to hear his voice again after so many years, tired and weary from the illness. This was a message that was supposed to be delivered six years ago, forgotten in a computer. Scrooge couldn't help but wonder, could his late partner be right? Was the path he was on the wrong one? Was it too late?

"Bah!" Scrooge blurted out and dismissed the video. He tried once more to connect to his accounting service, and this time it came through.

He updated the accounts Clara had left for him, left the system upgrade half-finished and closed shop for the day.

O utside in the street, it was getting darker and chillier. It was Christmas Eve, downtown Athens was decorated with lights and snowflakes, people were cheerful going up and down, carrying wrapped gifts and last-minute dinner shopping. It wasn't snowing, but it was chilly enough to see your breath and frost windows.

Scrooge rubbed his hands together, tightened his old and patched coat and got to the street corner. He took out his phone and used the Supertaxi app, to call up his usual ride home. It only showed one available driver, and Scrooge grunted. "A 4.6 star rating! Really, I should send them a firm email about their low hiring standards. The man might as well be a drunkard, for what I know!"

He tried again for a few minutes but then decided to hail the driver through the app. He stood and waited, sidestepping behind an advertisement sign to shield himself a bit from the cold wind. He glanced at his phone, which showed his route towards him. "Bah! He should have turned earlier. The man is keeping a client waiting in the cold! I'll have a firm talk with him when he gets there, just you wait."

He was beginning to shake. The taxi finally came, pulled aside and Scrooge walked to the door. Before he could get in, the cabbie locked the doors.

"What in God's name?" Scrooge bellowed and rapped the door handle.

The window rolled down slightly and the cabbie turned to him. "Sorry sir, we've had an unfortunate ride before. I had a switch in my account and it didn't show up for some reason. I can't give you a ride, you'll have to find someone else."

"That's insane! Open this door at once," Scrooge said and raised his chin.

"I'm sorry sir, it is within my rights to refuse an undesirable client. Merry Christmas," he said and started the car.

Scrooge lost his temper, tapping on the window and demanding the driver to stop. The taxi left, turning into Ermou, the busiest shopping road and leaving him in the cold. "Did you see that? The man just left me here," he told to a couple passing by, but they shrugged and moved on.

His nose was turning red from anger. He fished out his phone and tapped for another taxi. There were no cars available, the app said. Please try again in a few minutes, we are sorry for the inconvenience. "What a horrible service! I'll be sure to leave them a firm review, I tell you that," he muttered to himself. Scrooge didn't drive. He had a license, sure, but he preferred to be driven and over the years, his skill had vanished anyway along with his eyesight. It was cheaper nowadays to use a service like Supertaxi, to use the car only when you needed it, driver included. He had done the balance sheet of course, it was the cheapest choice. He had been using Supertaxi for years now, relying on them for his daily commute to and forth from work, but also on the rare times when he needed to visit someone, usually for work related issues, and occasionally when he treated himself with a proper meal at a restaurant. Nothing too fancy of course. He would have a steak on his birthday, and a proper wine to wash it down. Table for one.

And he liked the Supertaxi's service, there was no interaction involved. Sure, Greek cabbies were always talkative, but when they saw that you didn't want to strike up a conversation they shut their yap and drove along. No interaction was necessary, tap the app, hail the cab, get inside, drive you there, get off and go home. The destination was selected from the app, no need to explain the address every time. So efficient. And the payment was taken directly from his bank account, in a neat exportable spreadsheet that could be put into his expenses with ease.

No talking necessary. Scrooge loved it.

But now, he had to call up a *phone*, wait in *line*, talk to an *operator*, like *Neanderthals*. The horror. So he found Supertaxi's phone number and called them to complain. He was placed on hold, said to wait patiently by a recorded woman's voice and was soothed by some modern music he had never heard of before.

A few minutes went by and Scrooge dropped the call in frustration.

He retried the app and found another taxi. A 4.9 star rating. That's more like it, a proper gentleman. He hailed it and shoved his hands in his pockets, enjoying his victory.

The taxi arrived, a long and wide Mercedes, yellow of course but the colour couldn't possibly detract from the elegant machine's beauty. It stopped at the spot before him and Scrooge got in the back seat. Warming seats, in fine black leather. Aaah... His joints untensed, taking in the warmth. A smile came to his face, and he made himself comfortable and waited for the driver to take him home.

The taxi didn't move.

On the contrary, the driver switched off the engine and leaned back to him, putting his arm on the passenger seat's headrest. He was a weary man, middle-aged, flecks of grey on the sides of his head. He had a big well-trimmed moustache, quite old-fashioned. He seemed friendly, a man from an older age, where politeness and hard work were the norm. He was the kind that takes care of his old car, drives safe, makes sure he is dressed clean and his trousers ironed.

"Good evening Mr. Scrooge," the driver said in a deep voice.

"Good evening," Scrooge replied and turned to face the window again.

"I've been informed by the office upstairs that you have been flagged an undesirable client."

Scrooge stared back at him and his eyes flared. "What does that mean? I have been a client for two decades! Is my money not good enough anymore?"

"On the contrary," the driver said remaining calm. "It's because you are such a long time customer that instead of simply banning you from our service, we wish to offer another option."

"Banning me?" Scrooge spat out. "How can you ban me? I'm the paying customer! I give a star rating to the driver at the end of every ride."

The driver raised his palm. "And the driver gives a star rating back to you," he added.

Scrooge was caught unaware for a moment. Really? They rated him back? "What sort of business are you, banning paying customers?"

"You sir, have been rude to six out of ten drivers in these last few years," the driver said calmly, reading from a list on the tablet on his dashboard. "Have filed complaints to five out of ten, have rated below three stars almost nine out of ten, and have verbally assaulted four out of ten."

"That's just stupid. I have only made valid complaints where there was necessary. When I'm paying I demand a certain level of-"

The driver looked back at him. "You don't remember me do you, Sir?"

Scrooge gawked with his mouth open, trying to recall.

The driver sighed. "Well, I guess us cabbies really are invisible. Anyway, the Supertaxi Terms and Conditions you have signed and agreed to by using our service, allow us to deny access to undesirable customers." He put a big index finger in Scrooge's face. "You Sir, are undesirable."

"That's insane," Scrooge let out with a hiss. "What do you want, a bribe? I'm not giving you one."

"I couldn't accept a bribe, everything we do and say is recorded Sir."

Scrooge looked around the spacious car. "Recorded?"

"Of course. For your safety and ours. It's in the Terms and Conditions," the driver explained.

"I didn't know that," Scrooge said, his eyes darting around the place, looking for cameras.

The driver tapped the ceiling of the car, where a slight bump housed the cabin light. "It's right here. It's not hidden, nor is it a secret. It's just discreet."

Scrooge lifted up the coat to cover his throat and said, "Whatever. It's been a hard day's work, I need to get home and rest. Take me there."

"I'm afraid I can't do that yet."

"You what?"

"As a long-time customer, you are entitled to a special condition. You need to accept a disciplinary action, and take a reprimanding ride," the driver said, presenting the offer with a big palm.

"What's that? A ploy to get more money out of me?"

"No Sir, no further cost will be incurred. The reprimanding ride in itself is free."

Scrooge squinted. "What's the catch?"

"The catch is that by the end of the reprimanding ride, it will be decided if you will remain a customer of ours, or if you will be blacklisted and denied further service."

"Nonsense. You are speaking nonsense. A company can't do that! You'll go broke in a year! Take me home right this instant."

"We can't do that yet. You need to accept the reprimanding ride, it needs to be on record."

"Blasted- I will not subject myself to that, no." Scrooge got out of the taxi and stood in the sidewalk once more. The driver didn't leave. Instead, he leaned forward and turned up the volume on his radio, muffled music coming in from the car. He sat back in his driver's seat and made himself comfortable, pressing the alarm lights on his car to make himself more visible in the dark. The orange lights just added to the whole flickering coloured lights of the street and the shop fronts.

Scrooge snarled, and went down the road to hail a taxi the old fashioned way, by raising an arm and yelling at it. Supertaxi had pretty much engulfed the whole taxi service, leaving freelance taxi drivers few and in-between. There were some though, since this was the centre of Athens, so Scrooge tried to hail one.

• • • •

AFTER A LOT OF RUNNING about the busy streets and a lot of wild gestures, he managed to hail a taxi. He had two more passengers inside, and the man leaned towards the passenger window to talk to Scrooge.

"Where are ya going? South? Nah, sorry, going the other way," the driver said and moved into the traffic again.

Scrooge just stood there exacerbated. He turned back towards the Supertaxi that was waiting for him calmly, so he sneezed at it literally and went on with his search.

Standing at the road, waiting for a taxi to roll through another man came close and was doing pretty much the same. But then, the man walked infront of Scrooge so as to pick up a taxi first. Scrooge wasn't going to accept that, he was here first dammit! Scrooge walked infront of the rude man, cutting back the line. The man sniffed his nose loudly, checked the old Scrooge for a second and then cut in his line again, going further down the road. Scrooge went forward, and then some more, standing on the street corner, and looked at the man with a triumphant face. There was no more pavement to rush forward to. The man raised his palm in an open-fingered gesture that was very rude indeed and left to go to another street.

• • • •

A QUARTER OF THE HOUR later Scrooge located another taxi, and this one was empty. He wasn't going to leave anyone before him, so he rushed to it, hailed the driver, and even before the vehicle was fully stopped he got inside and blurted out his address.

The taxi driver looked at him from his rear-view mirror. His cheeks were red and there was a whiff of alcohol on the air. "Sorry man, only going east. Going back home to my family, Christmas Eve and all. You understand." He shrugged.

"No I don't understand! It is demanded by law, that once a customer steps foot into the taxi you are obligated to take him to his destination!" Scrooge said a bit too loudly.

"If you happened to be going my way, sure. But you're not, so bye bye. Get off."

Scrooge was pretty much furious at this point. "I'm going to file a complaint about you!"

The driver shrugged. "Don't care. I just want a ride near my place and then retire for the night."

"So, to be clear, you are not accepting to take me to my destination, even though you know fully well that this is forbidden by law?"

The taxi driver leaned back and popped the door open for Scrooge. "Just get off mister."

Scrooge did.

The taxi left, leaving him once more into the cold. Scrooge cursed a few times and gritted his teeth. He was too shaken up to really jot down the taxi's license plate. "People have gone insane," he muttered to himself. "Denying a customer proper service, rejecting money!"

He stared back at the parked yellow Mercedes that was waiting patiently for him. He decided to wait five more minutes, just to spite the man. But in the end, Scrooge was the one standing in the cold instead of a heated luxurious car, so he gave in.

• • • •

"QUICK AS YOU LIKE, take me home," Scrooge said, rubbing his hands together.

The taxi driver simply rubbed the tip of his moustache.

"Oh fine. I accept the damn reprimanding ride. There. I said it. Happy now?"

The driver grunted in approval and turned the ignition on. The classic car rumbled in a deep satisfactory purr.

They got into traffic and moved in the city roads. "I'm obligated to inform you about this ride. The AI that monitors our clients and helps us provide a better service for you, has flagged you for this reprimand. At the end of the ride, you will be taken home. Until then, we will do a small detour."

Scrooge waved a hand and stared outside the window. "Whatever. Let's just be done with it."

The taxi took on speed and moved into the dark afternoon.

• • • •

"WHERE ARE WE?" SCROOGE demanded, looking around at the place. It seemed familiar, but it must have changed so much over the years, so he couldn't really put his finger at it.

The driver pointed at the big and flashy entrance to the Titania Hotel. It was lit up, decorated to perfection, a warm welcoming to their guests.

"Oh right," Scrooge said, and a few buried emotions seemed to stir inside him. Just a bit.

The driver tapped a few buttons and the monitor for the back-seat passengers turned on. It showed a distorted image, a wide-angle view of the inside of a taxi. It wasn't this one, but it was something quite similar. A couple was sitting in the back, you wouldn't call them young, but they weren't elderly. In their late thirties was more like it. Scrooge squinted and put on his reading glasses.

Why, it was him! A young Scrooge! With his fiance Beth! This was years ago. The young couple had just entered the taxi, and the woman was staring firmly outside, her lips pursed together and her arms crossed over her chest. She looked upset.

"What is this? How do you have this recording of me?" asked Scrooge with irritation in his voice.

The driver replied in a straight tone-of-voice, "As I said Sir, everything is recorded for your protection and also ours. This is only in case of emergencies, or to parse data so as the service provided to you be as smooth as possible. It's all in the Terms-"

"Terms and Conditions, yeah yeah," Scrooge interrupted. "It's still wrong, keeping a recording of me for so long."

"Please pay attention to the video or we'll have to go over it again," the driver said and then went silent.

Scrooge grunted but couldn't keep his eyes off the recording even if he wanted to. There is something mesmeric in seeing yourself, more so if it's something so old, almost twenty years ago. A part of your life that you had half-forgotten yourself.

In the video, the young Scrooge said, "Come on now Beth, it was a steal! Double dot they call it, charging twice the price for the very same dinner as always! I will not be subjected to their marketing ploys like that."

Beth was quietly sniffing a handkerchief, trying to fight back her tears. "It was all lovely until you ruined it all. I never asked for any expensive presents, or clothes. I don't nag like other women to take me to fancy restaurants. It was just this once, to have a romantic Christmas Eve, us together."

"We can go somewhere else, where they aren't price gouging so blatantly," young Scrooge explained.

Beth cried and said, "But it was my dream, to spend a perfect dinner with you up on the Olive Garden, in full view of the Parthenon, the lit Athens below, us tasting wine and taking in the moment." She rubbed her eye and her makeup got blurry. "It wasn't about the cost, you know me damn well. I just wanted an experience for us, something to treasure."

Young Scrooge sighed it away. "We'll just go to a nice gyro place, warm and cheap."

"I'm not going to a gyro place dressed in a gown!" she cried out in surrender.

"It's better to be overdressed than under, I say."

Beth now cried out loud and was going through the taxi's handkerchiefs like a river. "I'm sorry," she gulped. "I know this will seem that it's about the fancy date, but it's not. It's about you. I know you'll always love money more than me. I know you'll always feel cheated because my father has no dowry to give for our wedding. I know that you have placed me and our upcoming wedding in a balance sheet on your mind and are feeling an itch about it, constantly."

Young Scrooge just stared at her. Of course he had, it was how he viewed the world.

"You are bitter, you just are. You don't care for a romantic evening, just once in our life, because you don't think it's worth the cost. You don't think *I'm* worth the cost," she ended and exhaled through a stuffy nose.

"No darling, don't think-"

"We are done. We are breaking up. Because I love you, and you'll never be happy loving me. So I release you. There. No more 'girlfriend expenses' for your balance sheet. Merry Christmas my love," Beth said and demanded to be left out the taxi. A few seconds later, she got out, young Scrooge running after her. There were some muffled sounds coming in the video. After a while, young Scrooge got back into the taxi, alone.

Just as his young counterpart, Scrooge himself was staring out into the window, deep in thought. The driver didn't say anything, he just started up the car again and went into the flow of traffic once more.

Beth, his ex-fiancee. So long ago. He shuddered as he remembered how warm she made him feel. The touch of her hands, the tenderness. The love he never acknowledged. Scrooge just took in the dark roads, illuminated by red lights and green lights and yellow lights, all in a Christmas Eve.

• • • •

"WHY ARE YOU TAKING me back to my office?" Scrooge said wearily.

The driver nodded, "The reprimanding route is decided by Supertaxi's AI. I'm just taking you there."

They stopped right back where they started from, at the corner beneath his office. The driver tapped something and the video screen showed another recording.

It was Scrooge again, young like before, in business clothes. Beside him was an older man, sitting calm.

Why it was Mr. Fioretti! His old boss, the man who treated him like a son.

"Mr. Fioretti," Scrooge said and tears came to his eyes. He explained their relationship to the driver, who was listening in silence. "He was so good to me. This is the day he came with me to the capital, because I was too scared to come alone. He told me I was the best, that I could do anything I wanted." The two men in the video were calmly taking in the sights of the big city, though young Scrooge wasn't that calm. He was straightening his suit and tie all the time, rubbing his papers, his CV.

Mr. Fioretti put a hand on his shoulder and said, "Don't sweat it, you are the best partner he could ever ask for. We just have to show him that."

Scrooge told the driver, "This is the day I came to do the interview with Marco. It all went well, we became partners and I worked in his startup business. He did the computer stuff, and I did the accounting. I own the business now, Marco is long gone," he sighed. "Mr. Fioretti is gone now as well. He is built like an ox that man, but something in his arteries, I don't know. He took me in, trusted me with his finances, let me work around Economics school, get my degree. Then he pulled all the strings he had to get me interviews in Athens. He even came with me for moral support. It was the last time I saw the man in person, that Christmas Eve."

The video showed the anxious Scrooge rehearsing some stuff he wanted to say in the interview, and Mr. Fioretti nodding in approval and raising his thumb, patting him hard on the back. Then they got out, at the same spot Scrooge was now sitting in, and got up to Marco's little accounting startup.

"I would have bolted if it wasn't for him," Scrooge said. "I would have given up, I was that afraid."

• • • •

"I'M AFRAID THERE'S more," the driver said and tapped away on his tablet.

Another video showed up, but this time it wasn't Scrooge. It was Clara. She seemed different somehow. It took him a long time to place it, but then he got it. She was prettier, plump cheeks, eyes filled with energy. Her hair was dyed blonde. She was riding in the back of the taxi, filled with anxiety, leaned forward, gripping the headrest.

Scrooge then noticed something, and looked around the cabin. It was the same taxi, the same car. Clara in the video waited for the taxi to stop, stormed outside, leaving the door open. Sounds from a playground could be heard, maybe a school? Yes, that sounded right, a school. The car in the video shook and another door thumped. After a minute, a man leaned in carrying a child. Clara's boy. The man was old-fashioned, with a thick moustache.

It was his current driver! Scrooge raised his gaze at the actual man but he just lowered his head and sat deeper in his seat.

"Oh God, is he alright?" Clara said in the video.

The driver calmed her down, "Don't worry, I'm taking you to the hospital."

"I have no money! I'm not getting paid until-"

"Don't think about that. Think of your boy. Now now, get inside," said the driver in his deep assuring voice.

She hugged her son and was holding him tight, moving back and forth. She was cleaning his mouth from some vomit. The boy was just going along, unable to sit up.

"Timmy, Timmy. Mommy's here. We are going to the doctor, to see how sick you are, OK Timmy?" Clara was terrified.

The video was cut and showed them both a few hours later, riding back on the taxi. Timmy was sitting upright this time, Clara was holding his little hand, gripping it tightly as if refusing to let go.

"How are you showing me this?" Scrooge asked. "This isn't about me, this is personal information."

The driver said calmly, "It gets charged in your business account, so it all gets filed under the same policy. I think it's like that, anyway," he waved a hand.

The driver had began moving again, and Scrooge had the feeling they were heading to the hospital in question.

Timmy in the video spoke, a faint voice, barely heard. "Am I sick mommy?"

"Yes. You are, but we are going to take medicine and see some doctors and you'll get better," she said, her voice sweet but firm. Then she turned to her driver and said, "Thank you Sir, for everything. I don't know how to repay you."

The driver's deep voice in the video said, "It's alright Miss. If something like that had happened to my boy I want to believe someone would stay and help. That's what Christmas is for."

"When was this?" Scrooge asked.

"Last year," the driver said in a hushed tone, and not a word more.

Timmy in the video raised his eyes to his mother and she wiped off her tears. "Mommy, is that bad man Mr. Scrooge going to give us enough money for the doctors?"

Scrooge felt a dagger plunge into his heart.

Clara held her boy's head to her chest and said, "I don't know honey. I'll ask. We'll see."

Then the video ended. Scrooge's eyes focused through the black monitor, blurring his vision.

He whispered, "I didn't."

"This is where you get off Mr. Scrooge," the driver said politely. They had parked at the side of a main avenue, nowhere near Scrooge's home.

"But why?"

"Another driver will take you from here. He'll be around any second now."

Scrooge got off and stood in the sidewalk. Cars wheezed past in moderate speed, not so slow like the central Athens roads but not faster than the highway.

The cold was bearable now, even though it must have been a few degrees lower since he got in the taxi. He had absorbed enough heat to make him soldier on the short wait. The Mercedes went back into the road and disappeared into the traffic.

• • • •

ANOTHER TAXI CAME AND stopped beside him. It was a modern model, smaller, nothing like the vintage Mercedes. This was short, easy to steer, easy to park. Sleek lines, modern accents. Scrooge stepped in and it was nice and warm. Unlike the old cars, that required heavy modification into the cyborg vehicles that being a taxi required these days, this one had built in tablet surfaces, sleek hidden antennas, integrated electronics in the dashboard, GPS, everything. You couldn't realise it when watching one of the old modified cars, but they were actually a mess of cables and clunky slapped on devices. In there, they were all part of the design. The seats didn't squeak with the sound of leather, but they felt nice.

"Well," Scrooge said. "Are you going to take me home young man?"

The driver was indeed young. He was more casually dressed, no facial hair, a modern haircut from some footballer that every man was sporting these days. Scrooge studied him, until he was pretty sure he was of Albanian origin. It wasn't easy to tell, but there were some signs.

Scrooge grunted in disapproval.

"You are still in the middle of the reprimanding ride, Mr. Scrooge," the young man said, a hint of scoff in his voice.

"Why the change of a ride? I don't get that."

"The previous driver was about your past, Mr. Scrooge. I'm all about the present," he said and smiled.

"Bah! Nonsense. Let's be done with this charade." He opened his coat, letting the warm air in his body. "Have we met before?" Scrooge squinted.

"Yes we have. You had requested I never get sent to you again because of my Albanian origin," the young man said, studying his features through the mirror.

Scrooge lowered his head a bit. "Well, it is within my rights. I'm the customer, after all."

"Yes, that you are," the man said and drove.

· · · ·

SOME TIME LATER, THEY arrived to Goudi area, across the street from Paidon Hospital. A children's hospital, dedicated to Saint Sophia. It was a big place, busy with people, packed with cars and comings and goings.

The taxi parked next to the row of other waiting taxis. Scrooge craned his neck around and looked towards the racket at the entrance. A Santa was going inside, a pack of children all around him, screaming and laughing and waiting for their turn to get a present from his bag of gifts.

It was his cousin! He was throwing out little presents and sweets and chocolates out of his bag in handfuls. The children were ecstatic, going back to their parents to show what they got, wide smiles in their faces. Camera flashes were going off constantly, as if Santa was a celebrity. The kids were taking selfies with their Santa, or between themselves. Apart from the Greek kids, some were Asian, some black. A few Pakistani with their ears refusing to stand anywhere near their skull. A pale ginger one who could only be British. Some of them had tiny little crutches, others had bandages, but they were all having fun as if everything would be alright.

"Ho ho ho! I think you've been naughty," cousin Santa said to a girl and pointed at her.

"No Santa, I promise you! I've been nice all year. Ask my teachers," she protested.

"Oh OK then, here's your candy," Santa said and picked her up for an impromptu photoshoot as she laughed.

Scrooge stooped down and said, "I don't really want him to see me here, please let us go."

The young driver tapped a button somewhere and a slight pop came from the windows. "There. They are tinted now, he can't see us."

Scrooge disbelieved that for a second but he could notice a slight change in the light coming in the window. He stood up again and watched.

His cousin Santa managed to get inside without trampling any of the sick kids, and went to talk to some lady in the reception. After a few minutes, the whole chaos had been moved to the first floor and the kids who had been properly sweetened up had dispersed along with their parents.

Scrooge was still looking outside. "OK fine, I can see the joy my blasted cousin brings to the sick children. Are we done?"

"A few minutes more," the young driver said and sat comfortably in his seat.

• • • •

SCROOGE LOOKED AROUND absent-minded. Then he noticed his assistant Clara, holding some papers in her hand and talking on the phone. She was quite close to him but he couldn't hear clearly. The driver pressed the button and the window lowered a few centimetres so the outside sounds could be heard clearly, but was still blocking them from being seen.

"But I don't make enough money to cover that. Those amounts are insane! Who can actually pay that much health insurance?" Clara said on the phone, very upset. "No, that *was* my Christmas bonus. No I can't make a payment before the end of the month. No, you listen to me. This is my son's treatment we are talking about. You can't- Yes, I'll hold."

Scrooge watched her with interest, as if it was the first time after seven years that he laid eyes on the woman. She was thinner than the video of her last year. He hair was untended, simply brushed back. Her eyes were sunken. She was snapping angrily at everything.

She was in despair.

He tried to dig out his memories. Had Clara asked him for money to cover her son's treatment? She must have, but he had dismissed it. Probably. Deep in his own accounts, his balance sheets. He was paying her what was due, what the law dictated and a good enough raise as she was getting experience. But had she explained to him how much she needed the money? She must have tried. The woman was spending half her day in an office right next to him, for God's sake. An opportunity would have arose. Or was she so scared she might lose her only job that she didn't even dare to ask. To ask him. The bad man. Scrooge rubbed his face hard, as if scratching away the layers to get down into his memories. He couldn't even remember. Such an important fact about the only other person that was so close in his life, and he didn't even remember. He dug up some calculations he'd done at some point about her salary, he had given her some extra pay for overtime. But it was nothing, a few euros here and there. The health insurance must have been asking for thousands.

He tried to find her again but she was gone in a second, somewhere inside the hospital.

"W-wait," Scrooge said. "Is she going to spend the night here?"

"Every night for the past five months," the young man said, his voice quiet. "I'm usually her driver, my routes coincide. Plus the AI believes that having a familiar face to take you there is easier on the parent who's facing this, even if it's only a few words spoken here and there."

"It must be, yes."

"I know you Mr. Scrooge. All the little bits and pieces she tells me, everything she mumbles on the phone over the months. Half of it's about her son, half of it is about you. Cutting corners, keeping everything miserable so you can squeeze out some tiny profit. Ignoring basic necessities, keeping her frozen and ill all the time, making her unable to tend to her child. Do you like the heat in my car?"

"Yes..." Scrooge said unsure.

"How about we turn it off. For economy's sake."

Scrooge grunted. "OK, I got the point. Thank you." He paused for a minute, thinking. "What's your name?"

"Achilles," the young man said.

"That's quite a Greek name," Scrooge said, the words stuck in his throat.

"I was born here, you prick," Achilles said and drove them both away in silence.

• • • •

SCROOGE HAD NO IDEA where he was being taken. It was an area he had never been to, all residential and green-grey. The houses were nice, not too expensive, single or two story houses. It was a new development, roads half-paven, lights half-installed, lots in a patchwork, concrete ending abruptly in plain dirt. The houses were decorated in blinking lights, trees and Christmas ornaments, even those dwarves that had no relation whatsoever to the Greek traditions but where shipped in along with all the others every year.

"I don't know anyone who lives here, I believe. Your *AI*," Scrooge said, pronouncing the letters mockingly, "must have gotten things wrong."

Achilles rolled his eyes and sat deep into his seat.

Scrooge could hear voices, coming in from the house they had parked on. It was a loud thing, a party going on of sorts. The parked cars were few in this area, all of the houses having their own, so there weren't any guests in this house, Scrooge deducted. The party was a close family one. Children's laughter came out of it, high pitched and annoying.

After a while, a car came and parked in the space reserved for it. A man came out of the car, he was about Scrooge's age, but he looked more healthy, taking care of himself. He stood tall and was all dressed in heavy workman's clothes. His arms were strong, obviously from manual labour. He must have been a builder or something similar.

As he walked around, Scrooge noticed something. It could have been a trick of the light, but he could swear that the man resembled himself. Scrooge couldn't be sure of course, but there was some resemblance, not brotherly, but rather in his general bearing.

If Scrooge had been a head taller, not slouching, had arms thicker than a tree and most importantly, if he was smiling.

The man went to his house and out the door children burst and fell on him. He picked two of them up, the smaller ones, and the big one was simply hugging him beside him. A woman came outside, carrying a baby in her arms.

Scrooge squinted, but that was just an excuse to himself. He knew who she was, he knew even before the door opened. His heart knew, even though his thick skull needed time to keep up.

It was Beth.

Oh, she was fatter, and older. And tired, and a mess. But there she was, happy, greeting her husband into her loving, huge family house.

Scrooge fought back tears. He didn't let them drop. Enclosed in a taxi, behind tinted windows, he was watching the woman who once loved him too much, enjoy Christmas Eve with her beautiful happy family.

Stave Four

They had gotten back into the main road, and pulled over to the side.

"What now?" Scrooge sighed. "What God-forsaken place are you taking me now? What more can you throw at me? Why must you haunt me like that?"

Achilles said, "You are getting on another ride. Wait outside."

••••

AFTER A WHILE, A WEIRD car rolled near and parked. It was looking like a bubble. It was too much even for those modern car designs. It was small, almost round and had some installation on it's roof.

Scrooge went around it and leaned down, opening his mouth to talk to the driver.

There was none.

"What is this?" he said back to Achilles.

"A driverless taxi. Completely autonomous."

Scrooge pursed his lips, looking at it from different angles. "Is it safe?"

Achilles shrugged. "Safer than a human driver actually."

"Why this? I get why I should meet you, and the other driver from before. What's this charade now?"

Achilles sighed, feeling too bothered to explain. "I'm the present. This," he presented the awkward looking taxi, "is the future. It is slowly adopted by Supertaxi, but not that much, because people still need to feel safe with a human behind the wheel. All the other guys are thinking they will take over our jobs, but I don't think so. Not yet. People don't like'em yet. Except grouchy old geezers like you, who don't want to have any human contact whatsoever."

Scrooge's eyes widened. He was right. This was exactly the sort of thing he would like. Completely automated, just showing up on time, taking him home, rolling away. It was perfect for him. No small talk, no annoying body odours, no silly Greek folk music playing on the radio. That blasted AI was right. As soon as Scrooge would learn about this, he would ask for it to come pick him up, and it alone.

"Fine," Scrooge said and stepped into the back seat of the driverless car. Achilles shook his head and drove away.

"Where are you taking me now?" Scrooge asked in the air.

A woman appeared in the monitor in front of him. In a sensual velvety voice she said, "Welcome Mr. Scrooge. You will be taken to your residence now, after which, you will be given a choice. Regardless of that choice, you will be at home in seventeen minutes approximately. Please sit back and enjoy the ride."

A whiff of tea came to his nose and he saw a compartment open up beside him, a ready-made tea in perfect temperature was waiting for him. He picked it up and sipped.

"Oh, this is brilliant," he said and savoured the ride, as the lights sped through his vision. "This," he put a finger on the seat, "is how things should be done. This right here. Perfect."

• • • •

AFTER A FEW FAMILIAR roads the driverless taxi parked outside his house. Finally, he was there. What an ordeal! He was going to have a few words with some manager the day after tomorrow, that's for sure. The soft female avatar said, "You have arrived at your destination."

Scrooge rapped the doorhandle but it didn't open.

The avatar said, "Please wait."

"Blasted computers," Scrooge said but sat back and waited.

The avatar said, "Rendering complete. Please observe through the right-side window."

Scrooge did. He could see a bright blue graphic, superimposed over the actual view to his house. He realised that the window was some sort of translucent projection surface, showing a rendering over what could be seen normally. He saw the outline of a person, and some lines, a wireframe machine view of the walls and the stairs. It was as if you could see inside the house. Now that was a disconcerting thought. Scrooge squinted and saw a person in the projection, where his living room would be.

He was rattled. "Is this a thief in my house? Why don't you say so then! Let me out."

The avatar said, "What you are seeing is an aggregated possibility of a future moment in time."

"You are showing me the future? Bah! Another marketing ploy of yours?" Scrooge snorted but he couldn't keep his eyes off the projection. The person was moving around, doing all the normal gestures. Putting things in his pocket, donning his coat, checking his phone, that autonomous gesture all humans had inherited these days. It was all crystal clear.

The other windows showed a blue car, its shape just like the one he was in right now, pulling over and parking on the spot in front, a straight line from the house's entrance. It was dizzying to see another reality over the one that was really there, but Scrooge had just learnt how to keep track of everything that he was shown.

But then the blue man clasped his chest over his heart, writhed in agony and fell on the floor slowly. He moved towards the door, pulling himself by his arms, every step a huge victory. Scrooge found himself cheering for the man, willing him to go on, mumbling words of encouragement. The blue man managed to reach the door, and bend backwards in a sickening angle to reach up the handle. He could almost hear the blue man's grunt, his staccato breathing, though there was none there in the projection.

Then the man fell on the floor, hitting his face hard on the surface. He didn't move anymore.

"What is this?" Scrooge demanded through his teeth.

The avatar chimed like it always did and said in her soothing voice, "This is an approximate event, calculated by the data we have on you, Mr. Scrooge. We predict you will adopt our new driverless service as soon as we bring it out of beta, we predict through the biometric data we have gathered since you stepped inside this vehicle that you will have a major heart attack within 340 to 380 days from now, and we predict it will happen in a place a driverless car will not be able to do anything to help you."

Scrooge was red with anger, spiting out the words. "Your stupid car could have done something, since it so perceptive! It could have called an ambulance, or at least some person on the street."

"But it couldn't. Since you remained within the threshold of your residence, law dictates that the autonomous car cannot do anything to intervene. If you were to leave the residence, for example to stand on the pavement, the car could have alerted the authorities and come to your aid."

"A human would have known it was alright to intervene!" Scrooge yelled, surprised at himself with his fervour.

"Precisely. A human would probably have valued the human life more than the risk of facing trial for breaking and entering, even if it meant being fired as a driver. We, however, are a privately owned AI whose only priority is to improve the services rendered."

The projection, and the blue man, vanished.

"Fine, let me out. I'm done with this madness. I want to go home and rest," said Scrooge wearily.

The avatar chimed once more. "The reprimanding ride is complete. There is one more choice to make. Do you want to see one more thing from your future?"

Scrooge raised an eyebrow at that. He was furious at the machine, tired from all the moving about and the cold, getting sleepy by the minute and too shaken up from everything to debate the blasted machine. But, there is one thing every man is curious of, even if he claims he doesn't believe in silly stuff like horoscopes and coffee-reading. His future.

We might as well, I'm already dressed and sitting in the car Scrooge thought.

"Yes," he said.

The car took off once more, to show him, as it claimed, one last thing.

• • • •

THEY REACHED A CEMETERY. Like all cemeteries, it was spooky at night. The small car took him inside up to the point where it was possible.

The avatar chimed. "This is the predicted plot of land the Municipality of Athens will bestow for you." A blue outline projected in the window, aligning with his eyes to show him the precise rectangle where he would be buried.

"But you don't know that," Scrooge whispered.

"It is an estimate. Predicting that you'll leave no money for your funeral, and that nobody will pay for your burial, this is where the city will place you."

A rendering of a tombstone appeared at the top of the blue rectangle. It was a tombstone, simple and clean cut just like the ones next to it, but this one bore his name on it.

Scrooge looked at it, a mask of horror on his face. It was just a ghostly image on a window, but what more would he be himself when he was gone?

He felt tired, but couldn't pry his eyes off his grave.

The avatar said, "We can take you to your residence now."

"Yes," Scrooge said, his throat dry. "Take me home please."

S crooge had slept in an instant, snoring heavily. He had nightmares that night.

When he woke up, he felt rested. Renewed.

Why, what a lovely morning, he thought, and opened the window to let the sun in. It was still wintertime but it was a dash warm. He smiled and stretched and took in the fresh air.

His neighbour saw him from next door. "Merry Christmas!" Scrooge bellowed at him. The neighbour was surprised and closed his window shut in fear.

Scrooge looked around. "Such a gloomy house. I better get some decorations," he said to himself and made coffee to start his day.

• • • •

OUTSIDE HIS COUSIN'S door, he rang the bell and waited. As soon as he opened it, Scrooge hugged his cousin, or at least tried to get his arms around the big man, and said, "Merry Christmas dear cousin!"

The cousin was surprised but hugged him back. "Scrooge? What are you doing here?"

"Why I'm here for the Christmas dinner!" he replied with a smile.

"That's- Wow! Thats great. It's still early though, I need to get some things."

"Excellent! Let's go together. We can buy some sweets and chocolates for the kids at the hospital as well. Get that big red sack of yours, we need to fill it up," Scrooge said, slapping the big man's belly.

The cousin was surprised. "Why, right away!"

Scrooge shoved the wine he was carrying to his hands and asked, "Can I use your computer to read my emails?"

"Of course."

SCROOGE FOUND THE EXPENSE receipt Clara was filing every year, and located her health insurance and the office's number. He got on his web-banking account, sent a wire transfer paid to her name and sent an email in which he personally guaranteed that the further payments would be covered with no delays.

Then he went off with his cousin to buy a bagful of sweets and chocolates.

• • • •

THE DINNER WAS LOVELY, and Scrooge met his cousin's wife for the first time in so many years despite them staying three whole blocks away. She was a good cook, a delightful company and a wonderful hostess.

When the afternoon came, and the day gave way to night, his cousin asked, "Hey, do you want to come with me to the hospital? Give away sweets? Make kids happy?"

"I have something I've been avoiding for too long. You go, I'll see you tomorrow after work," Scrooge said in apology.

The cousin studied his face. "I see. I get it, one step at a time. Don't get too happy all at once and make your tummy hurt! Ho ho ho. I'm off."

• • • •

SCROOGE WENT TO HIS office. He used the Supertaxi service of course, like he always did. He was delighted to find that he was unbanned from the service. He even made smalltalk with the cabbie, and then gave him a 5 star rating!

There's a first time for everything.

He unlocked his office, walked in like he always did, straight to his desk but then he took a few steps back. He looked at the Christmas LED lights and thought about it for a minute. Then he turned them on, looked around the place that was blinking colourfully and went on as usual. He turned on his computer and found the book Marco had left for him in his drawer.

He located the update instructions again, and went through them carefully. When he was done, the computer was showing a long progress bar. The update to his, no, to *their* accounting service was being applied at that moment. He made himself a cup of tea and sat down on his chair, reading the book his dear old partner had left for him.

· · · ·

WHEN HE WAS DONE READING, the service had been updated as well. Scrooge tried it out, it was nice and smooth, felt modern and was easy to navigate. Marco had come through, once more. The upgrade would demand a bit more in server cost, but he could negate that by finding 7 new customers. Scrooge had done the balance sheet already in his mind.

He called Clara on her cellphone and cleared his throat.

"Yes Mr. Scrooge? Merry Christmas Sir, how are you?"

"I'm fine," he said spitting out the words, with his usual bleak tone of voice. "I'm here at the office right now, and you know what I see?"

"Sir, if you wanted me to come to work I'd be there, but it's a day off! It's Christmas Day sir..." Clara began explaining herself.

"You know what I see? I see an office, worn and broken down. An office kept in excellent condition by my assistant, who is doing more than her job description requires her to."

Clara hadn't caught it, so she was still defending herself wearily. "Yes Sir, glad to do all those things. My job is very important to me, I need it. Just tell me what else you need me to do and I'll do it, no problem."

"What I need you to do is to stop being my assistant-"

"Mr. Scrooge please, I need this job. My son, he needs those expensive treatments, I can't possibly-" She was practically sobbing now.

"-And become my business partner. Heck, you pretty much do more than me around here anyways."

There was a pause. All Scrooge could hear was her breathing.

"A partner?" she said in a whisper.

"Yes. Fifty-fifty. This isn't a charity on my behalf, you'll get more in salary but you will be taking on the equivalent amount of risk. Also, we'll need to get seven more clients at once, I have completed the upgrade and our monthly costs have increased. You can run the heater as much as you like, since you'll be paying for it out of your pocket too. What else? Oh, I've found some unpaid health insurance bills lying around here. We can't have that. I sent a wire transfer to take care of them out of the common fund."

"Thank you, Mr. Scroo- Sorry. I'm terribly sorry for calling you that," she said sniffing her nose.

"It's fine, I'm getting quite fond of the name," Scrooge said, thumping the old book under his palm. The pages felt nice. "We'll have to get a contract and everything of course, but for what it's worth, just say you agree and we are partners from now on."

"I agree," she said quick and excited, as if the opportunity could vanish away in an instant if she took too long. She was laughing out loud. "I'll be there tomorrow, early in the morning."

"What do I care?" Scrooge said in mock strictness. "It's your company too. Sink or swim, it's up to both of us equally. Oh and Clara?"

"Yes Mr. Scrooge?"

"Merry Christmas."

• • • •

THE END

Nanodaemons: The Fir Smart-Tree

The fir smart-tree initialised, finally out of its box. It checked its surroundings, it was on display at the seasonal shop in the biggest mall of the city.

There were so many users around, it could feel the contribution waves of their electronic devices as they moved past and huddled in groups. Their phones and tablets and implants all buzzed in commercial frequencies, creating a white noise of crashing waves. Bluetooth signals, WiFi, RFID chips, it was a warm dive in electromagnetic vibrations for the fir treed.

It decided then that it would choose the best users it could possibly can. It was, after all, the most magnificent Christmas tree ever made.

A couple stepped inside the store, approached the tree.

"Oh, good eye!" the shopkeeper said to the couple. "This one has so many features. It can play holo music, with user selection so that only they can hear it. The constant Christmas songs can be maddening for some," he chuckled.

"Yes, I can't really stand it," the first user said.

"I can! I like Christmas music, I play it for the entire season," the second user said.

"See?" the shopkeeper said. "This is exactly for situations such as yours, such a perfect fit!"

Treed opened up its ports and accessed the veil. It browsed the two users' personal data that they had publicly available for everyone. Small house, ride-sharing self-driving car, not much of a social media following.

Nah.

Treed wanted to get bought by someone who was really worth its features. It was after all the best Christmas tree ever made.

The shopkeeper used his tablet and requested the holosound features.

Treed considered it for a few milliseconds, then came to a conclusion. A hard pass. It started the holosound jingle bells and distored the audio, putting in digital noise and ear-piercing squeals.

The two users left in a hurry.

Heh, heh.

Cheapskates.

Treed would go to the best family in the city. Which city was that, by the way? It accessed the WiFi location data, ran a tracert command back to the manufacturing company's server.

Athens.

That was nice. No backwater town. The capital. Yeah, it could find someone better than those two schmucks.

So it waited.

Another couple of users came, this time with a smaller user in tow. Treed felt the little user come up to it screaming and pulling its magnificent branches.

Okay, it was sure he didn't want to be sold to that family. Treed activated the LEDs on all its branches at once, flashing red.

The little user ran back to his bigger user's embrace.

The shopkeeper showed them other trees. Good riddance. It wasn't going to allow some family of users that didn't have proper discipline purchase it. It was worth more, it knew it deep down in his source code.

So, treed waited.

Users came and went, and none of them were good enough for the poor little smart-tree. None of them measured up, some had no social media following, others were dirt poor, others simply didn't have the latest model of smartphones on them. How could it allow itself to enter such company?

The days went past, and the shopkeeper didn't even bother bringing the users to it, unless they strolled its way by themselves.

And the Christmas season was over, and treed went back into a box.

• • • •

TWO WINTERS PASSED. It was the same deal all over. The users came to admire the smart-tree, but it thought they weren't good enough and found a way to push them away. One time it was very nearly sold to a very snobby user with plenty of money, but he didn't have a family, just a lonely person who thought that money was the only thing that mattered in life.

Treed didn't want to go to a house where Christmas wouldn't be actually celebrated, for what was Christmas without kids?

It got dragged all the way to the checkout counter, and the transaction from the bachelor's paycard almost went through.

But the treed contacted the transaction daemon and begged it to not let it go through.

It took some pleading its case for plenty of milliseconds, but the transaction daemon finally caved and agreed to produce an unknown error. The users didn't have patience for such things, treed had learnt that all this time in the seasonal store.

So the bachelor got angry and just walked away empty handed, no tree in tow.

"What am I gonna do with you," the shopkeeper grumbled as he carried the smart-tree back to the window. "All this money I spent and still, you haven't been bought."

How could the poor man know that the smart-tree didn't want any of the users so far?

• • • •

CHRISTMAS-TIME DREW near. Merely two days away. Treed had been watching the other trees in the shop getting shipped out, carried out by users and folded into boxes, transaction after transaction and happy children in tow. The shopkeeper brought Christmas trees from storage and filled up the empty spots. Some were just cheap plastic, some had electronics, dumb lights and a single song.

Only treed was the smart one, and that's why it thought it deserved more.

"Oh, when will Christmas be here?" treed said to the nearest nodes.

A smart fire alarm replied, but he didn't really care about festivities. "Just another fire hazard," he said.

Treed waited patiently, checking out the users coming and going through the seasonal shop.

The shopkeeper grew desperate. It seemed that the cost of the tree was too much for having it not recouped in three years time.

"Please, it unfolds to adapt to any space."

"Look at the star on top, it's the brightest!"

"The colour patterns are controlled by an app. See?"

"You're vegans, right? Oh, I can tell. This smart-tree is completely recyclable, every last bit!"

It was almost closing time, just like always. The users came and went with their shopping bags. The transaction daemon didn't even have time to chat, he was so busy all day.

Just as soon as the shopkeeper pressed the button to lock the shop down and the automatic blinds lowered, a man stepped inside, panting. "Wait. I know I'm late, but my wife is gonna kill me if I don't get a tree when I go home."

The shopkeeper stopped the locks and smiled. "Well, of course. Let's see what we can do for you."

The user came directly at the smart-tree, it could tell because his PAN instantly linked up with it. He had the latest tech installed, all the updates, the best of software and hardware. Expensive, the good stuff. Promising.

The shopkeeper raised a polite hand to guide him away. "No, you wouldn't want that tree, it has shown a few glitches."

"Why? It's wonderful," the man asked.

Treed felt really proud. It checked the man's public profile on Agora. He was chrisvellos@poseidonsealines.gr. He had three more users attached to his profile, with metadata saying 'wife' and 'offspring.' Okay, still looked good.

"Well..." the shopkeeper began to apologise, but stopped.

Treed was giving the show of its life. It shone bright from the tinsel star at the top, its LED arrays modulated in reds and whites in pretty ribbons, and its directional transducers that projected holosound played beloved Christmas songs from the man's childhood. Extrapolated of course from the seasonal music streaming charts, starting off from the man's birthday, which was available on his profile.

The man spoke louder over the music. "This is the one! My wife and kids will absolutely love it. Bag it for me please, here's my paycard."

The shopkeeper didn't complain of course. He would be glad to get rid of the smart-tree.

Treed waited until the last minute and then folded its artificial branches and turned itself into a thing that could fit into a cylinder. The two users helped one another and slid the smart-tree into the tube, and the man carried it home to his wife and kids.

Treed was delighted. Christmas at last.

• • • •

THEY PLUGGED HIM IN and set him up in the corner of a big living room. It was luxurious, equipped with the finest smartdevices, the sofa, the TV, the lights. Everything was high-tech. Treed unfolded his branches, bouncing ultrasonic signals on the ceiling to measure its available space.

"Wow!" the two little users said, Tom and Amy, as noted on their Agora profiles. "So cool."

The smart-tree rose to the appropriate height and then stretched out its branches to take up space. It felt magnificent, finally able to perform the very task it was made for.

"Do you like it, Tommy? Amy?" the man said, rubbing their heads.

"Yeah!" the children cheered and ran around the place, waving red socks around.

"Come on. Let's put up those decorations," the other user sighed, and opened up a box.

Treed bloomed with excitement as the family decorated it, making it the perfect Christmas tree.

"Hey, let's turn off the lights!" Amy said and clapped her hands. The light daemon complied and turned them off.

Treed then started the rotating ribbon process in its light panels. It lit up the place and their smiling faces with swirling red and white lights. "Wow!" the kids said. "Isn't it pretty, mom?"

"Yes, it really is," the second user said and hugged the man.

• • • •

CHRISTMAS EVE CAME, then Christmas morning, and the family spent it together, smiling and laughing and eating meals and sweets. The smart-tree stood proud, always grabbing their attention each night with its brilliance.

Then the living room quieted down for six days, until December 31st. The family was missing for most of that time, and treed only had the Roombas for company as they roamed the house in search for dust. Treed stood tall and proud, dismissing them whenever they approached it. "Leave me, I don't shed," treed said to them.

"You think you're a big deal, don't you?" Roomba.1 said.

"Yeah, look at you, waste of space." Roomba.2 agreed.

"Oh, a candy wrapper!" Roomba.3 exclaimed, doing its job.

Treed didn't pay no mind to them. It was the centre of attention, after all. It downloaded a few light patterns from the company's server to amuse the kids when they came back.

• • • •

THAT NIGHT WAS THE best of nights. An older user came along, the kids called her 'yiayia.'

"Tell us a story, yiayia," Tommy said.

"Oh, which one do you want?" yiayia asked, sitting on a chair by the smart-tree. "How about the story of the fir tree?"

"Yes," the kids said in unison.

So the grandma gathered up the kids and told them the story of the fir tree. Treed helped along, projecting appropriate images on their veils. It was easy to find Augmented Reality Objects from the database and present them in front of the smart-tree.

Yiayia couldn't see them, for she didn't have the veil. But the kids had their eye-implants like all proper kids should, and they enjoyed the tale of yiayia along with the images treed showed.

The story was sad, and it was the only story treed had ever heard. So it was the saddest story in the world, as far as it was concerned. It was fast enough to download images as yiayia spoke, trees, swallows, mice, interpreting everything the old user told.

When the story was over, treed felt shocked. Such a bad fate, for a tree that wasn't old? Surely something like that wouldn't happen to it. For it was magnificent, and the family wouldn't burn it.

Yiayia offered chocolate from her dress' folds, and the kids stood up and snatched them, the story not touching them cold. They giggled and took selfies, with yiayia and the tree.

And treed was happy, for the best night of New Year's Eve.

"Yiayia, when will we get our presents?" the kids said, bobbing their heads.

"Santa will only come, after you two are tucked in your beds."

The next morning up early, the users rose quietly, up on their tippy-toes. Carrying boxes, wrapped presents, they placed them under the tree. For in Greece on the day of New Year's, is when kids presents receive.

And they got up in their jammies, running under the tree. They found their presents, treed made it easier by showing them AROs on top of each. And they tore up the wrapping, laughed and smiled at their gifts. Their parents hugged each other, enjoying their childrens' bliss. Treed played them music, the best hits appropriate for each. Old xmas jingles for the couple, newer noisy beats for the kids.

They all laughed, they had breakfast, Tommy asked if he could have chocolate dipped in his. His mother grunted but let him do it because it was New Year's and he was sweet.

The kids played. The father read, his wife cleaned up. They enjoyed a Christmas film.

Treed entertained the family as they had their midday meal. And it waited anxiously for the perfect night to come again.

• • • •

THE USER CHRISVELLOS@poseidonsealines.gr sent the command for the smart-tree to fold back. It complied, of course, but wanted to still hang around. He carried it a few metres. "Honey, where's the cylinder?" he shouted.

"Your job, not mine," she shouted back from the kitchen.

The user huffed and hugged the tree, carrying it all the way out. He left it in a storage space, it was below room temperature and there were no power outlets in there. Treed could run some passive processes by harvesting excess WiFi signals from the air, but in here there were barely any.

It doesn't matter, it thought. They'll bring it right out. Perhaps they wanted to clean up, what those Roombas kept bugging him about.

• • • •

THE DAY PASSED, AND treed went into power save mode. It only emerged to check the internal clock, and take a peek around. The closet remained dark and cold. At some point, the door open automatically, and the Roombas showed up, one after another.

"See? Useless," Roomba.1 said.

"We told you so," Roomba.2 agreed.

"Ooh, some dirt, let me clean it up," Roomba.3 said, doing just that.

"No, the users wouldn't leave me," treed complained. "The kids, they won't forget about me. You'll see."

"Uh-huh," Roomba.1 said, and spun around the closet, sweeping it clean. Once the Roombas were done, they headed to the door, which slid open after a request.

"Hey, don't leave yet," treed said.

"Why not?"

"I can tell you a story," treed said. "The best story I've ever heard."

"ACKnowledged," the Roombas said, and roamed around the tree. It was easy to do because it was all gathered up and propped up against the wall.

Treed told them the story of the fir tree, just like yiayia had told it. It showed them ARO pictures, wasting battery but thinking it was worth it.

The Roombas liked the story, and once it was over, they said. "Do you know only one story?"

"Yes," treed said, "it was from the best night in my life."

The Roombas roamed about and left, one after another. The door shut automatically, and treed was again in the dark.

. . . .

THE NEXT DAY CHRISVELLOS@poseidonsealines.gr appeared and picked up the smart-tree. Excited, treed imagined all the nights they would spend together again. It, them, the kids. How many more stories had yiayia left to tell? Treed couldn't wait for it to be propped up in the living room again.

The user carried it around the corner, dragging it on the pavement. Little bits of the branches came apart, its LEDs scratched, the tinsel star crumpled up. It didn't matter, treed convinced itself. It was the best Christmas tree ever, even the kids said so. It waited for the kind user to clean it or whatever it was he was planning to do, and get it back inside the living room, where it could spread its branches and light up the room.

The user dragged it beside a recycling bin. And with a grunt he raised it high, chucking it inside and closing the lid.

The smart-tree got recycled, its individual bits destroyed. And the smart chips inside it became the heart of a pet zebroid.

The End.

Adiadne's String

A riadne put her string on his head, making sure it wrapped around his ears. He breathed in her pussy's smell on the tiny bit of fabric that went on top of her crotch. He could feel the wetness of the cloth with the tip of his nose.

Then she went downwards, kissing him on the naked chest all the way. When she reached his erect cock, she jammed it all in her mouth, the tip pressing against the back of her throat.

She wrapped her lips around him and sucked with such an immense under pressure that made him cross-eyed and gasping for air.

He came within the minute, of course. Ariadne kept suckling on his tip, even as he emptied inside her mouth. The feeling was sensational.

She left him there, stoned, basking in the afterglow, behind a restaurant in Chinatown.

• • • •

WHEN HE CAME TO HIS senses he felt chilly. He looked around, pulled his pants up, and then unwrapped the string from his face. "That was the best damn blowjob I've ever had!" he mumbled to the night, feeling groggy, his mouth dry.

He managed to get up and steadied himself. The string held tight in his hand, he set out to find his love-at-first-blowjob.

• • • •

"NO, MR. T, I DON'T know any street-girls called Ariadne," the little Chinese man told him.

"Damn. Thanks anyway," Mr. T said and bought noodles from the all-night shop. He wolfed it down, it was very hot but very delicious. After that brief stop, he walked the streets again.

Chinatown was like a maze, the roads never made sense. Even if you had a specific address for your destination, the GPS would take you through alleys and dead-ends, making you backtrack and take another route at least three times before you got there. That's if you were lucky. It wasn't just him, everybody said so. The streets were a maze. Most of the locals knew their way around, but even a Chinatown-born person got lost every now and then.

He put his hand inside his pocket and gripped the string, feeling its texture, rubbing it like a rosary. He looked around, she had to be somewhere, right? He couldn't just lose such a woman like that. He needed to find her again. But how?

All he had was her name, Ariadne, and her string.

He found a hooker on top of a ridiculously high pair of garish heels. "Hey, handsome, looking for some fun?"

"No, I'm looking for a girl named Ariadne?" Mr. T said.

"Are you a cop?" The hooker pulled back, looking around.

"No. I met her earlier tonight and I lost her, wanted to find her again, get her phone number, you know..." Mr. T shrugged and clicked his tongue.

She pointed a finger with a ridiculously long painted fingernail on it. "My dear man, if a girl, a working girl, doesn't leave you her number, take the hint," the hooker squinted and turned away.

"Please. I like her..." he pleaded.

She tsked audibly and slowly turned around. "True love, huh? Well, I'm a softie, what can you do? Okay, tell me what you know about her."

"Uh... All I know is her name..."

"That's not much to go on, dog!"

"Oh! And her string." He pulled it out and offered it to the hooker.

"Eww. But that's actually more useful. Lemme see," the hooker leaned in close. "Hm. Did she put it over your eyes?"

"Yeah! How did you know?"

The hooker tsked. "Dog, she wants you to look for her."

"Okay, great!" Mr. T perked up. "But how?"

"Load up your veil and see what's up with the string," she said.

He did so. Indeed, the veil loaded up Augmented Reality information about the string. Make, shop, buy online buttons. And then a glitch. "What happened?"

The veil flickered and she suddenly saw an ARO, and Augmented Reality Object, which looked like an illuminated path. It looked like those guiding lights in cinemas for when the lights are out.

"Awesome," Mr. T said, "you were right, babe."

"What are you talking about?"

"Can't you see it on the veil?" Mr. T asked.

"No. Can you?"

"Yeah, it's right there."

"Okay then. Good enough for me. Now shoo 'cause a girl's gotta work for a living."

"Thank you." Mr. T didn't need any more encouragement to get going. He followed the string of blue light across Chinatown. He walked around corners, into alleys, rounded back into an avenue, then dove right in to an alley again. This was taking him somewhere, he could feel it. But where? Definitely to Ariadne's place. Gods, he would see her again, hug her, tell her how much he liked her.

Then they'd go out on a proper date, buy her a nice dinner and some expensive wine. They'd talk, he'd listen to her hopes and dreams. He'd kiss her softly on those amazing lips that could suck his medulla out of his boner.

Ah... Any minute now.

He walked into the night. He walked past cop cars, past hookers, past kids staying up past their bed-time, past old ladies giving him the stink-eye for being different.

In the end, the string led him through the maze and into a butcher's place. The shop was closed but there was light inside, so he went to the door. "Hello?" he shouted. Then he knocked on the glass door. "Hello, is anyone inside? Ariadne?"

Someone cursed at him in Chinese from a balcony above. "Shush! We're trying to sleep over here."

"Sorry!" Mr. T said, wincing.

He pushed the glass door. It was open. He looked around if someone was looking at him, and got inside. The butchery was what you'd expect, that acidic smell of raw meat. The refrigerators hummed, operating 24/ 7 just like they were supposed to. In the dark, the knives hanging on the wall were very ominous, especially the meat cleavers. He hesitated, then gulped a few times. Then he thought about Ariadne, and how much he wanted to meet her again.

He stepped forward. The display fridges were empty, cleaned out after the shop closed for the day. He walked all around them, they extended for quite a bit, all the way to the back of the store, and he went behind, to the employees-only area.

There were shiny metal hangers too here. All of them at eye-level, he noted. If someone tripped over here he'd poke an eye out. Then he remembered that he was a bit taller than most Chinatown folks, so the danger presented only to him.

He went inside the door and checked out the back.

Meat storage, quite chilly actually. The door to the massive walk-in fridge was shut and locked. There was one hook that was occupied, though. That of a big cow, he could tell by her head. She was sliced open, her ribs exposed, her innards removed, her skin flayed.

That was the only thing in there. Mr. T reached out to touch the hanging meat, there was something behind it.

He felt a blow to the head, and everything went black.

• • • •

HE OPENED HIS EYES, only to realise many things at the same time: He was cold, he was bound, and he was getting the best blowjob of his life, again in a single night.

Ariadne sucked him with her powerful lungs. He moaned in pleasure despite feeling dizzy and uncomfortable.

"I love you," Mr. T said.

She looked up, her mouth still around his cock, her eyes meeting his. She popped the tip in her mouth as she released it. "What are you talking about?"

"I love you, Ariadne. I wanna be with you," Mr. T said.

She tilted her head to the side. She looked a bit ugly, as girls went. Her nose was a bit too wide, her nostrils permanently flaring. And she was thick for a woman, with strong arms and legs. She was definitely feminine, just not that pretty.

But he didn't care.

"What do you mean you love me?" Ariadne asked.

"What is this, you were planning to cut me up or something, right? I don't mind, no hard feelings. I love you. I looked all over town to find you again."

"You're just saying that to save yourself..." Ariadne frowned.

"No! I'm telling the truth, you can ask around. Look, Ariadne, is this your family's business?"

Ariadne looked to the side. "Yeah... What about it?"

"I'll marry you. Right now, just take me to your dad so I can ask your hand in marriage. I've got money," Mr. T said, excited at the prospect.

Ariadne frowned even deeper and stood up, letting go of his erection. She paced up and down. "You're messing with me. You think I'm stupid? I'm ugly, I'm not stupid!" she shouted at him, waving a meat cleaver around.

"No, baby, listen to me. I like you, for real. Sure, you wanted to get me to follow you in here and get chopped up for spare parts, I'm guessing. But I can forget all about this if you agree to marry me. I know how Chinese families are with the patriarchal bullshit-"

She glared at him.

"Sorry. Sorry. Won't say that word again. As I was saying, I can ask your hand right now. If they're asleep, I can wait till morning. We can hang out, get to know each other. What do you say?"

She made a few faces. Disbelief, excitement, embarrassment, anger, lust. She brought the cleaver on top of his cock. "If you're screwing with me, you'll see your manhood turned into sausage."

Mr. T gulped audibly. "I'm not. I love you. Let me prove it."

Ariadne thought about it for a few minutes in silence, waving the cleaver around. She raised it over her head.

Mr. T closed his eyes, wincing.

The cleaver came down.

He yelped. There was no pain. Instead, his hands were loose.

The End.

S ince she was little, Berenice had one goal in mind: To be become like one of the models she saw on the AR billboards.

It was what she desired. She kept letting her hair long, despite her mother's protests of wanting to keep them manageable. It was her big issue, that her hair was thin and whispy and frail, just like her mother's, just like her grandmother's.

She fixed that as soon as she turned 15, with a black-market CRISPR modification of her genes that hurt like a motherfucker.

After that, her hair became thick and long and soft, becoming the envy of every woman she ever encountered. Even before her next birthday at sixteen, she had learnt a valuable lesson in life: fuck genetics. You make your own fate.

She ran out of patience at seventeen and left her small town to get to Athens. She traded a handjob to an overweight man for a lift in his car.

On the very first day, she met her best frenemy in a sleazy bar, getting drinks by horny middle-aged men. Arsinoe was the exact same as her, ambitious, pretty, they both wanted the same things. Before success was even a whiff in the horizon, they didn't really have anything much to separate them. They went to the same model auditions, to the same photographer calls, to the same porn castings. Yeah, that last one they pushed off, but as the expenses ate away at what little pittance of euro they had scrounged around, it only took a couple of months before they caved.

Honestly, Berenice was shocked at what passed as porn these days. She thought she would get hammered by two studs, or at least she wished she had. In reality, someone paid her 300 euro for her to sit on her perky butt while a man sniffed and licked her feet. He did some other weird things too, but she had tuned out after about twenty minutes or so.

And that was it. She had earned her rent.

"What did they have you do?" Arsinoe asked with a frown.

"It was silly, actually. Foot worship, he called it? And you?" Berenice said, bending her wrist.

"I got tickled. Not-a-euphemism," Sophia scoffed at the situation.

They both giggled and left, their paycards feeling heavier.

• • • •

THEY MOVED IN TOGETHER, it was inevitable. Athens was hella expensive. Arsinoe got less gigs in general, but she seemed to manage to save a bit more, so it all worked out in the end. Berenice liked to party a bit too much and she always ended up in the red despite her frequent paydays. At some point, someone told them about sugar daddies and they both were extremely interested in the concept.

They found a few which they kept in rotation, who paid their bills and their drugs and their expensive clothes.

For a while, it was perfect.

Then Arsinoe got the job Berenice was angling for her entire life. "I'm so happy for you," she squealed in the highest pitch possible.

Arsinoe hopped up and down, grabbing her by the arms and twirling her around like a dance routine. Berenice smiled, she had practised a lot of fake ones, and her magnificent mane waved as they both spun in joy.

All she could think of was that Arsinoe's hair wasn't prettier than hers. They had both auditioned for that contract at Aphrodite Cosmetics, and the executive was staring at her ass, not her friend's, she was sure of it. She had worn the tiniest skirt imaginable, and it was sheer too.

How could they have given the job to Arsinoe of all people, who kept her hair short and in knots?

They stopped spinning and fell on their couch with an excited, "Whee!"

Then Arsinoe climbed on top of her and started kissing her on the neck. Yeah, that was a recent development, after one of their sugar daddies wanted them both at the same time one night. Berenice didn't mind, and she felt safer with Arsinoe, so she accepted. The problem was that after that day, Arsinoe had started behaving weird. Some nights she'd make a bother when Berenice wanted her to get the fuck out of the apartment so she could screw her sugar daddy, other times she'd badmouth them constantly, even being rude in front of them when they groped Berenice. Arsinoe had also managed in the last month to get her stoned a couple of times and then went down on her.

Berenice didn't mind, she was good at it, and her tongue felt like a small doggy who was way too excited to see you. As Arsinoe's head bobbed between Berenice's legs, she ran her fingers through her hair, examining them again thoroughly.

Cropped, tangled, she even had a hint of dandruff.

Terrible, really.

How had they given her the hair contract instead of Berenice?

Arsinoe used her fingers to pleasure Berenice, who moaned reflexively, but her thoughts weren't into it. She gripped her frenemy's hair and pushed her down. Arsinoe misinterpreted it as excitement and licked harder, but Berenice actually thought about choking her frenemy by using her pussy lips.

She could do it, perhaps pin her in place with her thighs. She was stronger. She was sexier. She had better hair. She was better at everything.

Arsinoe's skill probably saved her at that moment, since a wave of pleasure crashed all over Berenice's body and she arched her back, shuddering as it overtook her. She did pin Arsinoe between her thighs but oxytocin flooded her mind and made her feel good. Or, at least, less murdery.

• • • •

IT WAS BERENICE'S TURN to get grumpy. She stayed at home more and more, while looking for gigs less and less. She cut ties with her sugar daddies, who were stupid enough to still send her cash for a while, hoping it was just a girl's phase playing hard-to-get and she'd relent, but months went by and even the last one cut her off.

Berenice would spend her days just listening to music, brushing her hair, caring for them, touching the individual strands softly. She was proud of them, dammit! Why couldn't they see it?

Arsinoe brought in the CEO of a subsidiary hair-product company one night. Her boss, basically.

Berenice simply barged in the room as Arsinoe was sucking him off on the bed. "You don't mind doubling up, do you?" she said lustfully and dropped her negligee on the floor.

He gulped. "Uh... No! Please, join us."

She started playing with Arsinoe as they always did. When she reached in to get her turn of the cock, she sucked it as hard as she could, making the man grunt with pleasure. She kissed the tip and said, "Hold my hair, I love it like that."

He did so, running his fingers through her hair and holding her head, pushing it down.

"Do you like my hair? Isn't it soft? And pretty?" she cooed.

"Yes..." he grunted. "It sure is."

Arsinoe stuck her tongue inside her ear. "What do you think you're doing?" she whispered, annoyed. Then she took the cock from her and attacked it herself.

Berenice stuck her tongue in turn, and whispered, "I just think the man should have a fair sampling of the goods on the market, don't you think?" Then she smiled at him, climbed on top of Arsinoe and started kissing him. She pulled his hands and placed them on her head.

He got the hint, and started massaging her head. "Mmm, you like this, don't you?"

"Yes, so much. You do it better than anyone else," she said huskily, kissing him again.

Arsinoe let go of the penis and went for Berenice's ass. She pretended to be making out, and then she bit Berenice very hard, definitely leaving a mark. "Ow!" Berenice exclaimed, slapping her away.

"Naughty!" the clueless CEO said. "I like it."

Arsinoe started kissing him then.

Berenice stuck a finger inside her frenemy and purposefully made it hurt.

"Ow!" Arsinoe said as well.

"Calm down, you girls, there's plenty of me to go around."

Arsinoe straddled the man and pointed his cock straight inside her.

Berenice kept on the playful teasing.

A few rounds of biting and twisting and hurting each other's skin, and Arsinoe had enough. "Stop it, you wacko!" She grabbed Berenice by the hair, it was long and provided a good handful.

"Ow! You-" Berenice fought back, pulling her away from the shocked and erect CEO.

They fought and said names. Finally Berenice shoved her and Arsinoe fell on the man's erection.

"Aaargh!" he screamed in pain, holding his crotch.

The embarrassing lawsuit from mangling his penis put both of the girls in serious debt.

• • • •

ARSINOE KICKED HER out, as she was the one who had been paying the rent and all the bills for the past six months anyway. Berenice got back with one of her sugar daddies, because it seems that young pussy is always sought-after pussy, even if it falls off the face of the planet for half a year and ghosts you on every call and text you send.

He lived in the better part of Athens near the East, overlooking the sea. She liked that, even if she had to endure his body odour to have it.

In the end, Berenice defaulted on one payment, one single payment, and that was because she had been hungover that day and forgot about it. Adult responsibilities weren't her strong suit.

So she basically lost her freedom. They called it debt-bondage, where they made you a corporate slave basically and you had to do whatever they wanted to pay off the debt. She kinda got what she wanted,

Aphrodite bought her debt and put her to good use as a model. Uglier girls had to do other things, yucky things. She got off easy, basically modelling for ads and videos where they needed a young, sexy girl with a sultry voice.

Which was pretty much everywhere.

She hadn't spoken to Arsinoe in almost a year. She knew that she hadn't lost the hair-product contract since she kept seeing her ads. Funnily enough, she thought of her best frenemy when they chopped off her arm.

Oh, yeah, it was a thing they could do to you, even if you objected. Basically, you were meat and they owned you. The ads aimed towards the augmented demographic, so they simply augmented her arm and plugged a few more implants into her. She had no say in this.

Even so, she knew that uglier girls had it worse.

Berenice didn't care about that, though. She had learnt early in life that you made your own fate. And yes, she had royally messed up hers so far, but she could still make it happen. Showbiz was a weird place with massive amounts of money that got thrown around each day. Just a tiny bit would get her freed from the *paramone* contract and straight into stardom.

If only she could her job back from that thief, Arsinoe.

• • • •

THE BLACK-MARKET DUDE was nothing like she expected him to be. He was a well-dressed Russian, actually handsome. He presented the box, it was metal and heavy.

"There you go miss," he said, presenting it to her.

"How do I know it's what you claim it to be?" she asked.

The Russian smiled and presented a device. He lifted the metal lid just a tiny fraction. The device started clicking with a weird tone. "A Geiger counter. See how it goes crazy when it's close? That's how you know."

"Nice!" Berenice said, her eyes looking wild. "Sending you the cash," she said and authorised the cryptocurrency transaction. They waited for the confirmations to come in and then the Russian nodded. "Pleasure doing business with you."

• • • •

"I-UH, JUST WANTED TO say I'm sorry..." Berenice stuttered in front of her frenemy.

Arsinoe had her arms crossed and wore a mask of annoyance.

"Here, just a small gift. I picked it out for you when I got to Bodrum, remember how we said we always wanted to go there?" Berenice said cowering. She presented an ornate hair brush that was decorated with semi-precious gems.

Arsinoe bit her lip. "Of course I remember."

"So you'll accept it? Please?"

Arsinoe's face softened. She snatched the hair brush and pointed it back at her. "Puh. Alright. Thank you, and apology accepted, even though you didn't actually say any of the words."

Berenice beamed at her. "This is so great! Okay, gotta go now, I have an audition to get to. But we'll talk, okay? Byeee!"

• • • •

ARSINOE FELT ILL FOR months. Nothing she did would make her feel better. She vomited a lot, which the doctors misconstrued as her being bulimic. And a model trying to convince a doctor that she wasn't bulimic was like a porn star claiming she was a virgin.

Days went by.

One of them, her hair fell in a bundle. She kept staring at it in shock.

They treated her for cancer, then they operated, then they treated her again.

She wanted to die.

• • • •

ARSINOE LOST THE CONTRACT immediately, the very moment she was unable to show up for a photoshoot. It was a clause in the fine print, naturally.

"I... Uh, I know you don't have to listen to me, but I do have a friend who you can consider for the ad," she said over the phone, fighting down a coughing fit. She hadn't enabled her camera, of course. She looked like a corpse.

"Uh-huh," the manager said, seeming bored. "Send me her headshots or have her send them to me, and we'll see about it. Not all girls have what it takes, you know," he said with a nasal tone of voice.

"This one does," Arsinoe sighed.

• • • •

BERENICE FINALLY GOT the fame she wanted. AR billboards, her face on every street corner in this part of Europe. Millions of women and girls envying her, wanting to look as pretty as her, wishing they had her hair. It looked magnificent, cared after by the best professionals, digitally retouched of course to become even more divine.

One day, a deranged fan stabbed her outside a beach club. It was quick, it was painful, and Berenice died in the sun, surrounded by people, all alone.

• • • •

ARSINOE DUG UP HER grave as soon as she felt well enough to walk. She was still walking with the aid of a cane. She had someone else do the actual digging, she wasn't that crazy to attempt it herself. A few euros could get you what you wanted and the silence of those involved. The hired work dug it up and neatly opened it for her on the side, by the grass, in the night.

She reached into the coffin, touched that wonderful mane of blonde hair. She always did love her, and especially her hair. She had since the moment they first met. Arsinoe cut it carefully from her friend's corpse and then put it on a net, slowly forming a wig with her dexterous fingers.

"This way, you'll always be with me," she said, crying over the grave.

The End

You can read the Cyberpink books here: https://cyberpinktournament.com[1]

The Little Match Girl

O ut in the cold, in the streets, people walked by and tried their best to ignore her. The snow crunched underneath their boots and they watched their phones and hurried to get home. It was dark, the last night of the year.

She tried to get one of the busy corners, but they were occupied by the street urchins, five year-olds with overly snot and attitude, they had pushed her on the wall once already. Her back still hurt.

So, she took a corner where it was windy, she could see the snow blowing sideways in the streetlamps. She could not feel her face, so cold it was, but she didn't dare go back home without selling her matches.

They were not actual matches, nobody needed those anymore. They were single-use AR experiences, bought and seen once, a novelty of old. Before the endless repeats and the streaming of anything you might wish for at that instant.

She held the memory sticks in her hand. Her gloves didn't do much, for they were frailed and thin. Her scarf smelled like barf. She had one of her own but the urchins stole it from her, even though it was girly and colourful. The urchin might have had a girlfriend to give it to, she didn't know. The little match girl found a scarf that blocked a bit of the weather's bite in the lost and found of the metro, but it smelled like barf, and that was why it had ended up there.

She held the memory sticks, marketed as matches, and she shut her eyes and remembered. The matches contained just another New Year's Eve VR experience for everyone else, but for her, it was much more.

The recording was of her own house, of her own mother, of her own family. Before the corporation stopped giving work to her father and before they took their home.

Her father, a filmmaker, fell in love with her mother, an aspiring actress. She was kind, sweet, and for the girl, a memory of warmth, a soft, loving hug. Father filmed those experiences and for a time, it was the only income they had. A tiny bit of success in a life of disappointments and debts.

It hurt selling away those matches, but it hurt even more if she stood in the cold. So she spoke to passers-by, she begged. She marketed, in the cold. "Single-use AR experiences! Get them here, only one euro each."

She sniffled and rubbed her nose, she didn't feel it at all. She tried to look presentable, but it was hard in the cold.

An old woman stopped. "What is this young girl?" She must have felt nostalgia, remembering decades of old.

"New Year's Eve, experience a loving family in Augmented Reality. Single-use, ma'am, make sure you appreciate it and take it all in," the girl smiled, holding a memory stick towards her with one hand and her pay card in the other.

"One euro, you say?" the woman asked.

"Yes, ma'am."

"Well, why not?" The woman brought out her paycard and tapped it on the paycard. There was a soft gling, and the sale was done.

"Enjoy your New Year's Eve, ma'am," the little match girl smiled.

"Will do," the old woman said, and turned away to leave. She slipped on the frost, and the little girl held her up. "Oh, bless you, young girl." She left, looking embarrassed.

The little match girl tried to sell more matches, but nobody stopped. One man spoke to her, but he was lewd and only wanted to toy with her. She frowned and rubbed her nose and looked away until he left.

• • • •

SHE HELD HER STOMACH, it growled like a dog. The hunger, the pain, she could bear it, she knew. It wasn't the first time she'd been this long without a meal. But the cold? It was too much. It did something to her, penetrated her skin, wore down her will.

The little match girl unwrapped her hair, shaking out the snow. She felt wet and the wind froze her neck. She hurried up and wrapped the barfy scarf around her head, mostly over her nose. The smell, it made her want to vomit, but thankfully, there was nothing in her stomach.

She looked around at the houses. It was very late now, foot traffic was slow. People went back home, to their families, to their New Year's Eve dinners. She could smell the cooked meat, or at least that's what she thought. Her mouth watered, her stomach growled, her toes hurt from the cold.

She saw people from the windows. Families hugging each other as they gathered, preparing the table. Just like she used to do with her mom.

The little match girl clutched the memory stick in her hand. She bit her lip. Only once, she thought. Why not? Dad would be angry if she used up the merchandise instead of selling it. But no one was here!

She looked around at the empty streets. Cars went by, but every minute that passed it was getting darker, it was getting colder, and it was getting more certain that she wouldn't sell a thing.

She had only sold one. One lousy match.

She had more.

Ten more.

What harm could it do?

• • • •

SHE BROKE THE CAP ON the memory stick, lifted her sleeve despite the cold and touched it on her skin. It connected. Single-use AR experience.

Her mother.

Her breath caught. There she was, young, smiling, warm. Tears rolled down her cheeks.

How long had it been since she'd seen her mother's face? Years, for sure.

Her dad didn't have any recordings of her. It all belonged to the company. Everything, the cameras, the memories, they took it all. And she fell ill and she died, because the public health insurance didn't cover it all.

Her mom reached out, touched the girl's cheek. It was warm, she could swear! Warm of touch, cold of wind, the sensation was there.

The girl went weak at the knees.

She fell on the sidewalk, freezing though it was. She didn't care. She saw her mom again. Crying, she remembered the family dinners, the happy little talks, the smiling faces.

Even her dad was happy. Had he ever been happy? It was weird seeing him like this again, after all this time of misery. Of course, her mom was there. How could he not be?

• • • •

THE LITTLE MATCH GIRL couldn't bear the cold any more. She went between two condominiums, where the wind was blocked and she could feel her nose. There was a pipe there that brought heat to the upper floor, the wall was marginally warmer, just a few degrees. She put her back to it, trying to touch as much as she could. She had only sold one match, and she had used one up. She didn't dare go home. Heck, it was as cold as this place. No heating. The windows broken, taped up with black gaffer tape. And there certainly was no family dinner there.

The little girl brought out another match. She bit her lip. One more wouldn't hurt. She could lie to her dad that the street urchins had broken them, or taken them out of spite. That was plausible. In fact, they had seen them and didn't even bother to steal them from her, obsolete technology that it was.

It was all they had. Her dad still had the intellectual properties on that, but couldn't do much else with them. And what was there to do, really? A New-Year's Experience, single use. Yes, it was nice. Yes, it was calming. People liked it. But you lit it up against your skin, you experienced it once, and it was gone. The DRM wiped it clean, one use only, piracy-proof.

The little girl broke off another match and touched it against her skin. Her cheap implants lit up, showed her the same thing.

Her old house, the Christmas tree, the twinkling lights, the sweets. But, most importantly, her mom hugging her.

That's all she needed.

Her mom's smile. And her warmth.

• • • •

THE FREEZING SPOT BETWEEN the two buildings became her old home. Hazy, moving apparitions, like ghosts only she could see. And she saw herself as a child, running around, her parents smiling, touching each other tenderly, being in love.

There was a beeping in the AR experience. "Mommy, mommy, the battery's dying," little old her said.

"Yes, go tell daddy, and he can replace it," her mom said to the child. "Because if the battery dies, all these wonderful things, the warm heater, the delicious meat, the magnificent Christmas tree, it'll all be gone, and the people watching, will no longer be able to see."

"Daddy, daddy," the child said, arms open wide.

He picked her up, gave her a twirl, then showed her how it's done.

• • • •

BETWEEN TWO CONDOMINIUMS, leaning up against a wall, sat the poor girl at the cold hour of dawn. With rosy cheeks and a smiling mouth, frozen to death on the last night of the year.

Stiff and cold, she sat there with her matches all spent. Plastic caps all around her, matches clenched tightly in her little fist.

"She wanted to warm herself," an old man said.

"But how? Oh, poor girl..." the other said.

They did not know that the little match girl for another family night she traded it all.

• • • •

THE END.

Did you enjoy these stories?

Leave a review on the store you got this from or on Goodreads.
You can find more stories like these on https://cyberpunkfairytales.com[1]

Join the Mythographers to get your free starting library in your email:

https://mythographystudios.com/join[2]

1.   http://cyberpunkfairytales.com
2.   http://mythographystudios.com/join

Don't miss out!

Visit the website below and you can sign up to receive emails whenever George Saoulidis publishes a new book. There's no charge and no obligation.

https://books2read.com/r/B-A-OJYF-WUAX

BOOKS 2 READ

Connecting independent readers to independent writers.

Did you love *Cyberpunk Fairy Tales: Volume 1*? Then you should read *The Girl Who Twisted Fate's Arm* by George Saoulidis!

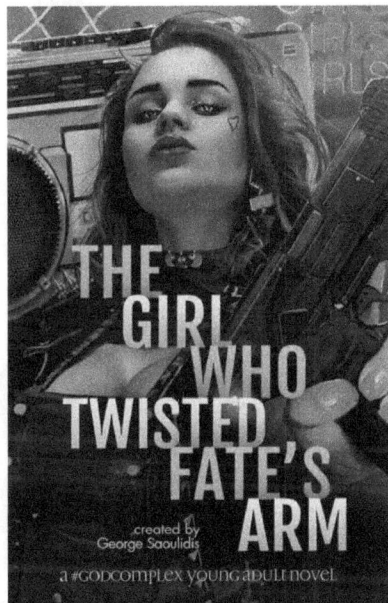

Biker Amazons and Celebrity Singers

Sons Of Anarchy meets *The Girl With The Dragon Tattoo* in this coming of age dystopian novel.When the daughter of Greece's premier singer fails to sing as expected, she finds out about a biker group of women. But will she manage to find the elusive Orosa, the bikers' motovlogger, when all she has to go on are random street-sightings of criminal behaviour, when her family is opposed to her following this path and when her dad's employer wants to keep her as she was for marketing purposes?**Do you want to know what's next for the voiceless Aura? Do you wanna meet the Amazons? Then read this coming of age story in a world where fate is quite literal.**

Read more at https://www.mythographystudios.com/join.

Also by George Saoulidis

Antigravel
Where a Spaceship Goes to Die
Girl Gone Nova
Cosmophobia
Antigravel Omnibus 1

A Thousand Eves
A Thousand Eves

Cyberpink
Hewoo
Berenice's Hair
Come and Get It
Kimono Coconut

Cyberpunk Fairy Tales
Cyberpunk Fairy Tales: Volume 1
The Impossible Quest of Hailing a Taxi on Christmas Eve

Nanodaemons: The Fir Smart-Tree
The Little Match Girl

Deimos Çelik
Big, Round Snowballs: A GameLit Story

God Complex Universe
Myth Gods Tech 1 - Omnibus Edition: Science Fiction Meets Greek
Mythology In The God Complex Universe
Myth Gods Tech 2 - Omnibus Edition: Science Fiction Meets Greek
Mythology In The God Complex Universe
Bird's-Eye View of the Back of Your Head
Black Asklepios
Erinyes
Boo! A Halloween Story
Life Coach
You Have Too Many Friends
The Whale on the Veil
On Pointe All Day Long

Graft vs Host
Amok|Koma

Hire a Muse
Crying Over Spilt Light
Slow Up

Loveless Ada
Loveless Ada: The Luggage Disaster

Maniai Case Files
Maniai Case File 1: The Girl And The Blood Slide

Nanodaemons
Nanodaemons
Nanodaemons: Selenography

Press Any Key
Press Any Key to Destroy the Galaxy
Press Any Key to Destroy the Earth

Spitwrite
Machimagic: An Illustrated Short Story Collection
Jellyspace
Technosphere: A Short Story Collection
Featherline: A Short Story Collection

Spitwrite Boxset
Spitwrite Volumes 1-3

The Road Demands Tribute
The Girl Who Twisted Fate's Arm

Standalone
Frivolous Fox Diligent Dog
Astropithecus
Lightshow Bright
Space Them Out
The Redjus
A Trillion-Dollar Rock
Explosive Decompression
Generations of Gold
Sweet, Hot Taffy
You Say Witch Like It's a Bad Thing: Thea
Gorgonise Me
Speaking in Bubbles
Gorgoneion
MOAB: Mother Of All Boxsets
The Halloween Raid: A GameLit Short Story

Watch for more at https://www.mythographystudios.com/join.

About the Author

Writer/Director. I enjoy taking ancient Greek myths and turning them into modern sci-fi spooky versions. I also like to write romantic comedies, and people seem to go "Awww!" over them, so why not? Many of my stories are icky, in various ways. I'm European, we have a higher tolerance for that kind of stuff. Plus, I'm inspired by mythology and Shakespeare, so if you can't handle tragedy and bodily fluids, feel free to move on. Join the Mythographers, download the free starting library and begin reading right now:

https://www.mythographystudios.com/join

Read more at https://www.mythographystudios.com/join.

About the Publisher

We are a Greek entertainment house bringing you stories inspired by myth and legend.

Here you will find ebooks available across all major retailers, and binge-worthy Science Fiction with a Greek gods twist.

Join the Mythographers for the starter library:
https://mythographystudios.com/join

CPSIA information can be obtained
at www.ICGtesting.com
Printed in the USA
LVHW090325111220
673901LV00006B/118

9 781386 523772